**Canadian Cataloguing in Publication Data**

Julian-Ottie, Vanessa
Sebastian, the tale of a curious kitten

ISBN 0-590-73376-1 (bound) ISBN 0-590-73377-X (pbk.)

1. Toy and movable books. I. Title.

PZ7.J935 Se 1989    j823'.914    C89-093647-1

Designed and produced by Mathew Price Ltd. for Scholastic-TAB Publications Ltd., 123 Newkirk Road, Richmond Hill, Ontario, Canada L4C 3G5.

Printed in Hong Kong for Imago Publishing Ltd.

# Sebastian

## The tale of a curious kitten

*VANESSA JULIAN-OTTIE*

SCHOLASTIC

This is Sebastian, always the odd one out, heading for the cat flap. "Where are you off to, Sebastian? Come back!" called Mother Cat.

Sebastian paid no attention.
He was already outside,
sniffing new smells and
hearing new sounds.

"What's that? Who's there?"
Sebastian gathered up his paws
and jumped through the hole
in the rocks.

"Ow! Ow! Ow!" cried Sebastian.
"That hurt!"

Sebastian limped towards the fence.
He felt cross.
"Just a minute," he said, "what sort
of animal is that?"

"Hello," said the goat.
"Hello, hello," said the ducks.
"Where are you going to?"
But Sebastian crept by and never
said a word. He felt silly.

Beyond the duck pond was a drainpipe.
Sebastian looked and looked.
Was that a mouse at the other end?
He pounced.

*Kersplosh!*
Where did that mouse go?

Sebastian found the mouse
in the barn. He crept forward.
He didn't know somebody
was watching him.

"Help!"
He'd never seen a horse before.
Don't worry, Sebastian,
he won't hurt you.
But what's that behind you?
Look out!

Sebastian ran for the gap
in the old stone wall
as fast as his legs could go.
"Arf! Arf!" panted the terrier behind him.
"Arf! Arf! Arf!"

Sebastian squeezed through just in time.
He headed straight for home and never
saw the rabbits who had been playing
hide-and-seek in the garden all day.

He didn't stop running till he got to
his own front door.
He could smell something delicious
coming through the cat flap.

Mother Cat was glad to see him back, and
he was just in time for dinner.
He felt warm and comfortable.
It was good to be home.